Yawning
in Assembly

Written by
John Townsend

Illustrated by
Rory Walker

There was a young teacher who swallowed a fly.
I think I know why she swallowed the fly.
She yawned in assembly.

There was a young teacher who swallowed a spider.
It wiggled and jiggled and tickled inside her.

She swallowed the spider to eat the fly.
I think I know why she swallowed the fly.
I hope she won't die.

There was a young teacher who swallowed a bird.
Oh my word – she swallowed a bird!
She swallowed the bird to eat the spider
that wiggled and jiggled and tickled inside her.

She swallowed the spider to eat the fly.
I think I know why she swallowed the fly.
I hope she won't die.

There was a young teacher who swallowed a cat.
She got very fat when she swallowed the cat!
She swallowed the cat to eat the bird.
She swallowed the bird to eat the spider
that wiggled and jiggled and tickled inside her.

She swallowed the spider to eat the fly.
I think I know why she swallowed the fly.
I hope she won't die.

There was a young teacher who swallowed a fox.
It caused a few shocks when she swallowed the fox!
She swallowed the fox to eat the cat.

She swallowed the cat to eat the bird.
She swallowed the bird to eat the spider
that wiggled and jiggled and tickled inside her.

She swallowed the spider to eat the fly.
I think I know why she swallowed the fly.
I hope she won't die.

There was a young teacher who ate a hyena.
Her face turned greener as she swallowed the hyena!
She ate the hyena to eat the fox.
She swallowed the fox to eat the cat.

She swallowed the cat to eat the bird.
She swallowed the bird to eat the spider
that wiggled and jiggled and tickled inside her.

She swallowed the spider to eat the fly,
I think I know why she swallowed the fly.
I hope she won't die.

There was a young teacher who brought home a tiger.
Lucky for her – it lay down beside her …
(And it went to sleep as it wasn't hungry.)
I don't think she'll die.

The moral of the story is:
NEVER YAWN IN ASSEMBLY!